To the children and teachers
of Montessori de Terra Linda School,
and to educators and children everywhere.
D.M.

To Chuck—
thank you for believing in me.
T.T.B.

QUEST
FOR THE
CRYSTAL CASTLE

A Peaceful Warrior Children's Book

Dan Millman

Illustrated by
T. Taylor Bruce

H J Kramer Inc
Starseed Press
Tiburon, California

After breakfast, on a Saturday morning near the end of summer, Danny Morgan turned on the TV. His dad turned it off. "You know the rules, son: No television until the afternoon."

"But there's nothing else to *do* around here!" Danny grumbled.

"Sure there is," his father replied. "First you can put your dishes in the sink and take out the trash. After that, you'll think of something else—"

"Can you play catch with me, Dad?"

"Sorry, Danny. I'd like to, but I have to finish a report before lunch." Then his father went into his office to work.

Disappointed, Danny pushed open the kitchen door, dropped his dishes in the sink, and carried the trash out onto the porch. He heard his mother call to him from inside, "Danny, why don't you see if Carl or Joy can come over?"

"They're still at summer camp," he replied. "Mom, when can *I* go to camp?"

"Maybe next year," she answered.

"Everything's next year," Danny muttered to himself as he sat on the front steps and sulked.

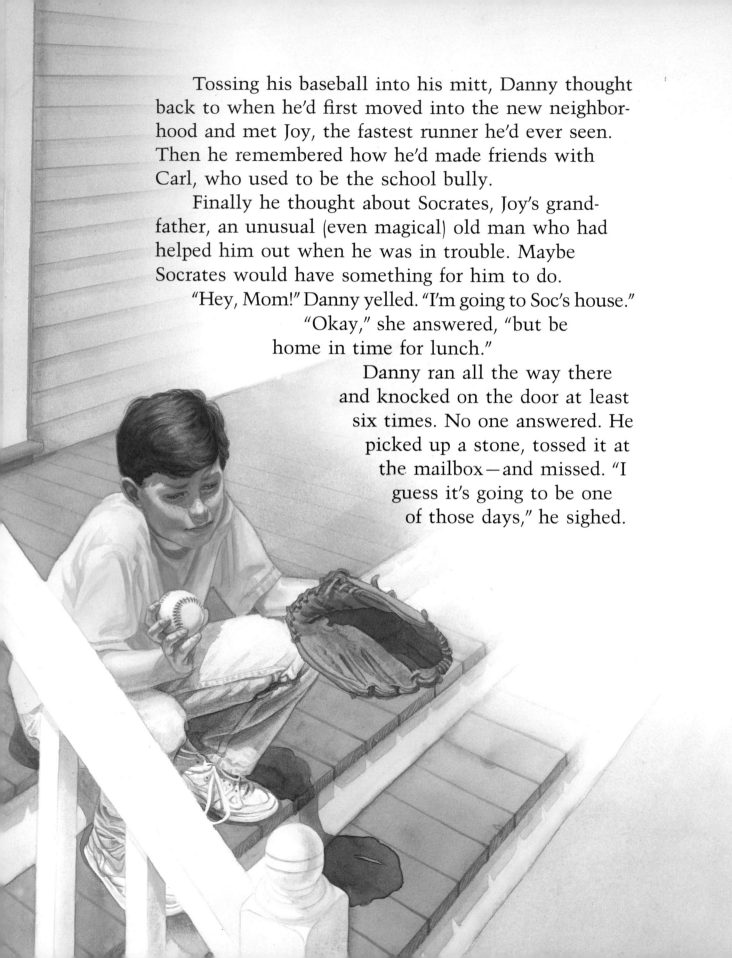

Tossing his baseball into his mitt, Danny thought back to when he'd first moved into the new neighborhood and met Joy, the fastest runner he'd ever seen. Then he remembered how he'd made friends with Carl, who used to be the school bully.

Finally he thought about Socrates, Joy's grandfather, an unusual (even magical) old man who had helped him out when he was in trouble. Maybe Socrates would have something for him to do.

"Hey, Mom!" Danny yelled. "I'm going to Soc's house."

"Okay," she answered, "but be home in time for lunch."

Danny ran all the way there and knocked on the door at least six times. No one answered. He picked up a stone, tossed it at the mailbox—and missed. "I guess it's going to be one of those days," he sighed.

Danny walked slowly toward home, up over the grassy knoll called Frenchman's Hill. As he neared the top and walked past a large boulder, he almost tripped over Socrates, lying on his belly, peering at the ground. A canvas knapsack lay across his shoulders.

"Socrates!" Danny said brightly, glad to see his old friend. "What are you doing here?"

The old man smiled. "Looking at these little guys," he replied. Then he turned back to the ground.

Danny knelt down and peered at the little creatures. "Just some ants," he shrugged.

"Not *just* ants," Socrates replied. "Look closer—it's a real bug adventure. Those little guys are trying to carry a huge bread crumb back to their hole. Let's see if they make it."

Danny lay down for a closer look and asked, "Why don't you carry it for them—put it by their hole?"

Socrates shook his head. "I don't think so—no need to interfere with nature."

"It's not interfering; it's helping," Danny suggested.

Socrates paused, then asked, "Did you know that if you help open the shell of a chick about to be born—if you don't let it peck its own way out—the chick dies?"

"*Really*?"

"Yep," Soc replied, watching the ants at work. "Sometimes, helping too much isn't really helping at all."

Nodding, Danny hugged his knees. After a moment of silence, he asked, "Socrates, when you were a kid, did you ever wish you were somewhere else—somewhere more exciting?"

Socrates turned and stared at Danny. Then, abruptly, he stood. "If you're looking for excitement somewhere *else*, there's something you need to see."

"I hope it isn't more bugs," Danny joked, following Soc up the hill.

As they climbed higher, Danny noticed something strange: Frenchman's Hill was little more than a big pile of earth, hardly taller than the housetops. But now they were climbing higher than he had ever been before—up into a cold gray mist so thick that Danny could barely see his own feet.

What seemed like hours later, they emerged from the fog and stood on a lofty peak overlooking miles of dark forest below in a valley Danny had never seen before. There was no sign of his home, or of the world he knew.

Squinting in the bright sun, Danny turned, and
saw behind him an old gray castle, still and lifeless,
worn by the winds of time. All that remained was
one wall, a crumbling tower, and an old drawbridge
splintered with age.

"Where are we?" asked Danny, bewildered.

"In a different world," Socrates replied. "Would
you like to explore?"

"Well, sure!" he answered. But just then, another
sight caught Danny's eye. "Socrates, look!" he
exclaimed, pointing toward a distant mountain
peak. There stood another castle, glowing
like an emerald flame—the most beautiful
sight he had ever seen.

Socrates glanced at the distant
castle, then back at Danny. "It appears
you have a decision to make: Stay
here, where you are, or go on a
quest to the crystal castle."

Danny looked back at the old castle, then turned toward the distant mountain. As he gazed at the shimmering towers of emerald, he heard the faraway sound of bells. He seemed to remember those bells and a magical castle calling to him from a dream.

Danny looked up at Socrates. "I'm supposed to be home for lunch," he said.

"You will be—*if* you survive the journey," Socrates replied.

"What do you mean, *if* I survive?"

"You'll reach that castle only at the end of a long and difficult quest. Many dangers await you in the shadows, and I won't be around to help."

"You're not coming?" Danny asked, feeling a sudden chill.

"No," Socrates replied. "Some things we have to do alone. And," he added darkly, "once you begin, there can be no turning back. You *must* reach the castle before you can find your way home."

Danny held his breath; a part of him wanted to go, but another part was afraid. He looked once again at the distant castle, bathed in sunlight—then down at the dark forest. "I'll go," he said firmly. His courage had overcome his fear.

"So be it," Socrates replied, removing his knapsack and handing it to Danny. "All the supplies you'll need are inside. Keep them safe."

Danny peered into the sack and discovered a knife, some food, a canteen of water, matches, a jacket, and a piece of flint. He heard Socrates say, "No matter how tough it gets, always remember that you *chose* to make this journey."

When Danny looked up, the old man was gone. "Socrates?" Danny called out. The only answer was the gentle sigh of the wind.

As Danny descended into the shadow of the trees that grew on the far slope, a cold wind bit into his bones. He put the jacket on. Suddenly the grade became steeper. He tripped, stumbled forward, and then lost his footing altogether as the earth gave way beneath his feet. Down he fell, sliding, tumbling head over heels, grabbing at branches that broke away in his hands.

Finally, Danny came to rest at the bottom—bruised and covered with dirt. His knapsack had ripped open, scattering his supplies somewhere on the mountain above.

Wiping the dirt from his face, Danny noticed that only the piece of flint remained in his ruined pack. Without thinking, he slipped it into his pocket.

Socrates had told him there was no turning back. But now, hungry, sore, and discouraged, he felt like he had failed before he had even begun.

"Got to stay calm," he said. "Find out where I am and where the castle is."

Danny looked up into the giant trees overhead. "I'll have to climb. It's the only way." So, panting with an effort that made his muscles shake, he climbed the tallest tree he could find. Swaying on the uppermost branch, he caught sight of the castle shining through the mist.

Danny broke off a dead branch, threw it to the forest floor as a pointer, and then descended. At least now he knew where he was going. But it was so far! How could he ever make it without food and water? Fear began to creep into his mind.

Then he remembered something his dad had said to him once: "You can accomplish *anything* by taking one step at a time." And so, Danny took his first step.

At first, broad forest paths made
travel easy; Danny walked on a soft
carpet of leaves and pine needles. But
soon, the way grew narrower and darker.
Cut by thorns, his body aching, growing
weak with hunger, Danny fought his
way through thick bush and tangled
brambles.

The faint cry of birds was the only
reminder of life in the forest.
Then the bird cries disappeared,
and only his breathing broke
the silence.

Near nightfall, just as Danny entered a small clearing, the sun dropped over the edge of the world, and the cold descended like a curtain. "Got to make a f-f-fire," he stammered. He knew he would freeze if he didn't. He gathered some moss and dried twigs, and set them up like a little teepee. Then, with fingers so numb he could hardly feel them, he searched for the flint, and found it, tucked away in his back pocket.

He struck the flint against a stone again and again. "Come on, come *on*," Danny said. At last, in the darkness, a bright orange spark fell into the dry moss. He blew carefully and saw a puff of smoke. Then a small flame came to life.

A few minutes later, warmed by the fire, Danny lay curled up and cozy in a bed of leaves. He was hungry, but he was warm and glad to be alive.

Gazing into the crackling flames beneath a starry sky, thinking of his friends, his parents, and the everyday world he had left behind, Danny Morgan fell asleep.

Danny awoke to an icy dawn, as a cold drizzle drowned the last embers of the fire. Chilled to the bone, he got up and started running to stay warm. "Got to find food," he said to himself as he ran. "And get out of this rain."

Panting, Danny found an old hollow tree trunk. He sat huddled inside, shivering, hugging himself, waiting for the rain to pass. And as he sat, he remembered how upset he had felt when his father had turned off the TV, and how he'd sulked about simple chores like wiping off the table and taking out the trash. Now he doubted he would ever see his home and family again.

Just then, voices began whispering from the trees and inside his mind: "You're spoiled . . . lazy . . . weak . . . ungrateful . . . you don't deserve to make it . . . give up . . . just quit. . . ."

Danny pushed on through the rain, trying to shut out the voices, but he felt so weary he could hardly put one foot in front of the other. The forest was drawing the life out of him; the voices were stealing his energy.

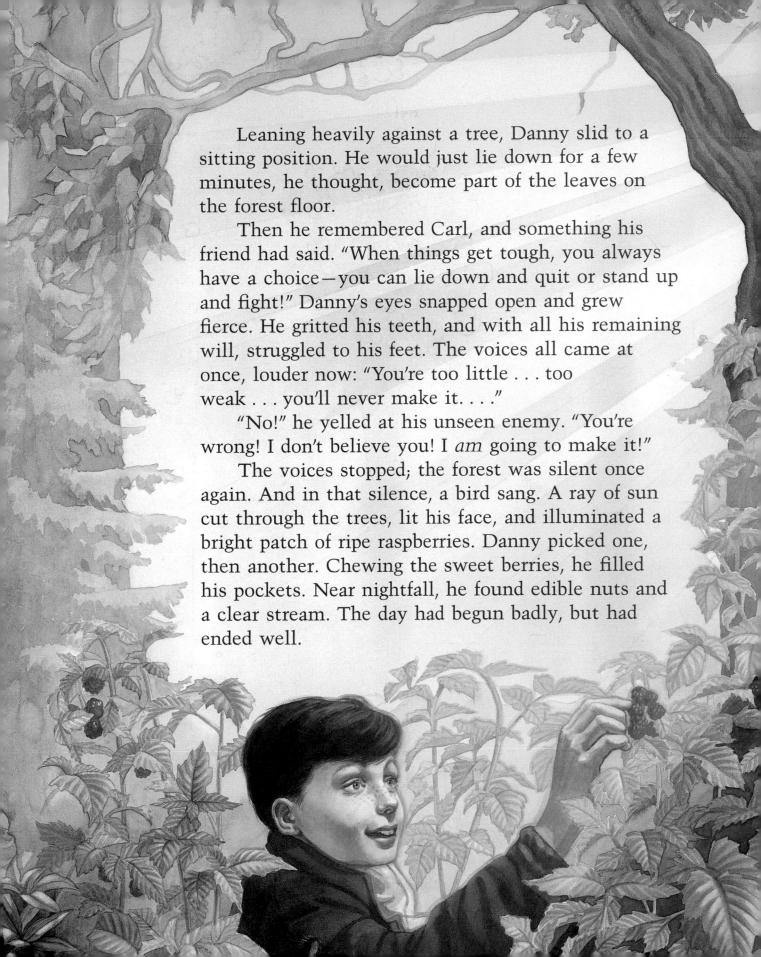

Leaning heavily against a tree, Danny slid to a sitting position. He would just lie down for a few minutes, he thought, become part of the leaves on the forest floor.

Then he remembered Carl, and something his friend had said. "When things get tough, you always have a choice—you can lie down and quit or stand up and fight!" Danny's eyes snapped open and grew fierce. He gritted his teeth, and with all his remaining will, struggled to his feet. The voices all came at once, louder now: "You're too little . . . too weak . . . you'll never make it. . . ."

"No!" he yelled at his unseen enemy. "You're wrong! I don't believe you! I *am* going to make it!"

The voices stopped; the forest was silent once again. And in that silence, a bird sang. A ray of sun cut through the trees, lit his face, and illuminated a bright patch of ripe raspberries. Danny picked one, then another. Chewing the sweet berries, he filled his pockets. Near nightfall, he found edible nuts and a clear stream. The day had begun badly, but had ended well.

The next day's journey took Danny to the edge of a deep canyon. His eyes traveled down the sheer cliff walls to a shallow stream rushing past far below. Somehow he was going to have to get to the other side, but it was at least twelve feet across—too far to jump.

He looked left and right; the canyon stretched as far as he could see in both directions. Walking along the edge, searching for a way around, he was startled by a voice calling to him. "Help! Help me!"

Peering across, Danny saw his friend Carl clinging to the face of the cliff. It didn't seem possible, but there he was! "Carl! It's me, Danny. I'll get you— hang on!" He searched even more frantically for a way to cross.

"Danny, I'm slipping!" Carl yelled.

"Hold on, Carl, hold on!" Danny's voice echoed off the canyon walls.

There was no time to think. Danny had to act or his friend would fall. Backing up for a running start, he focused on the other side of the canyon.

Joy's face flashed into his mind. "Go for it!" she cheered. And so, running with all his might, he came to the edge and leaped, soaring into the air. But then Danny began to drop like a stone. He wasn't going to make it.

But he *had* to!

His only chance was a tree root, growing out of the cliff. He reached for it.

Danny caught hold of the tree root. With a surge of strength, he scrambled up onto solid earth, rolled quickly toward Carl, and leaned over the edge. "Carl, grab my . . ."

Carl was no longer there; in his place sat a brown bear cub, whining softly, its hind paws slipping from the precarious perch.

Mystified, Danny reached down and pulled the little bear to safety. The cub looked up into his eyes, and a voice spoke inside Danny. "Kindness begets kindness," it said. Then the bear disappeared into the forest.

And so Danny continued on his quest, living on berries and what nuts he could find. He grew accustomed to walking for hours at a time, with short rests in patches of sunlight. His feet were sore, but he felt himself growing stronger with each passing mile. And, slowly, the crystal castle grew nearer.

Several days passed. Then, late one afternoon, Danny heard a loud crackling noise and smelled fire—not a camp fire, but the choking scent of a forest fire. The sky filled with black smoke and screeching birds. Deer, rabbits, and other small creatures leaped past him, frantically running the other way. Fanned by the wind, a wall of flame rolled toward Danny like a red-hot tidal wave. The entire forest was ablaze.

Just then Danny heard a voice. As he peered ahead, the smoke cleared and he saw someone, almost engulfed by the flames. "No. It *can't* be," he said. Squinting into the approaching fire, he saw *Joy*—lying on the ground crying out to him, her ankle caught in a tree root, struggling to free herself.

Danny started toward her, holding his hands
up in front of his face. He fell back as a wall of heat
struck him. Then Joy's scream pierced the air, and
Danny found himself running into the flames. He
couldn't breathe; the air itself was on fire. His eyes
were almost swollen shut. But somehow, he made his
way toward her. "Joy!" he called out, dropping to the
ground. But his only answer was the pitiful cry of a
hawk, its leg tangled in a tree root, flapping its wings
in panic. Joy had disappeared.

Dazed, Danny freed the bird's leg. Instead of
fleeing, the hawk sat very still, stared into his eyes,
and spoke inside his mind: "Kindness begets
kindness." Then the bird soared
into the sky.

In that instant, the fire and the forest itself vanished as if they had never been. Danny found himself in a meadow surrounded by fresh blossoms of every color. The cool air had a sweet fragrance. "This is a very strange forest," Danny said as his eyes rolled back in his head and he fell unconscious to the soft grass.

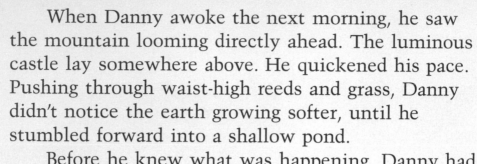

When Danny awoke the next morning, he saw the mountain looming directly ahead. The luminous castle lay somewhere above. He quickened his pace. Pushing through waist-high reeds and grass, Danny didn't notice the earth growing softer, until he stumbled forward into a shallow pond.

Before he knew what was happening, Danny had sunk up to his waist in a pit of quicksand. He tried to escape, but couldn't; the quicksand held him.

He sank deeper with every movement. Soon his chest was covered. He grabbed a reed. It broke off in his hand. "Think!" he told himself. "Fight! Don't give up!" Lifting his chin out, he spied the low hanging branch of a nearby tree. He pulled his weary arm free, reached up, and grabbed it.

Danny's hand began to slip; he started to panic. Then he heard Soc's words echo in his mind: "No matter how tough it gets, always remember you *chose* to make this journey."

With a burst of strength, Danny reached up with his other hand and began to pull himself out. "If only the branch holds!" he prayed. Slowly he rose out of the slime. Then, just as he pulled free, the branch broke. Danny plunged back and sank beneath the surface.

In the blackness, he felt a tug on the branch; he held on tight. The next thing he knew, he was being pulled out of the quicksand, up onto the solid earth. Coughing, he wiped the sand from his eyes, looked up, and saw a mother bear and her cub disappearing into the forest. "Kindness begets kindness" sounded in his mind.

A short distance away, he found a fresh, clear pond and cleaned the caked sand from his clothes and body. Refreshed, Danny continued on, and when darkness came, he stopped and fell into a deep sleep.

When he awoke, the sun was shining brightly on the mountain cliffs towering above him. Somewhere in the clouds, the crystal castle waited. Without delay, he started to climb.

At first he found many ledges and cracks to use as handholds and toeholds. But as he climbed higher, Danny found himself hanging onto a cliff wall by one hand and foot, searching in vain for another handhold. His fingers ached, and the wind began to blow.

A rock beneath his foot jarred loose, almost taking him along as it went crashing hundreds of feet down to the boulders below. The wind tore at Danny's clothing. He started to slip; this time, there was nothing to save him.

As if in slow motion, he fell backward. He saw the faces of his parents, Joy, Carl, and Socrates as he somersaulted through space toward the rocks below.

The next moment, as if by magic, he felt himself
slowing down, held aloft by a cloud of hawks. He
heard the soft flapping of many wings, as they lifted
him up into the sky, up toward the mountaintop.

The birds gently laid him on a carpet of soft grass
in a high meadow shrouded in mist. "Kindness begets
kindness," he heard them say in a corner of his mind.

Danny said a silent thank-you as the birds filled the sky and were gone. Then he stood, took a deep breath, and turned toward the shimmering outline of the castle now only a short hike away.

When Danny emerged from the mist, he let out a disappointed gasp. The castle before him was not made of crystal, but of old, crumbling stones, like the one he had left behind many days before. What had looked like an emerald flame was the sunlight, reflecting off moss-covered stones wet with dew.

Then, from nowhere, Socrates appeared and placed his hand on Danny's shoulder.

Surprised to see his old friend, Danny cried, "Socrates—the castle, it's not made of crystal at all!"

Soc knelt down next to Danny. "Yes, I noticed that, too," he replied, pointing back toward the mountain where Danny's quest had begun. Shocked, Danny saw the faraway vision of a beautiful castle, shining like the purest crystal.

"Things often look better in the distance," Socrates said. "And sometimes it's hard to appreciate what we have right in front of us."

"Then it was all for nothing," Danny said, disappointed.

"All for nothing? No, I don't think so. Look at yourself—look how tall you're standing. You've *changed*. And what you learned on your quest I never could have taught you at home. So *what* if there's no pot of gold at the end of the rainbow? The rewards of the journey don't lie at the end, Danny. *It's the journey itself that makes the warrior.*"

Danny looked at himself in the reflection of a pond. Socrates was right. He had changed. He stood taller. He felt older, stronger, and wiser. He had found out he was capable of more than he had ever imagined.

"Socrates," Danny said smiling, "I'm ready to go home."

Smiling back, Socrates pointed to a nearby tree. "The apples are ripening," he said, starting to climb. "Let's pick a few."

Suddenly hungry, Danny climbed up after Socrates, found a perch on a sturdy branch, and bit into the crisp, juicy fruit.

"You know," Danny said, glancing around, "this looks a lot like the tree in your yard."

"Is that so?" said Socrates. Then, smiling mischievously, he hung from a branch and dropped out of sight.

Danny jumped down, too. "I mean it . . . it really does look . . ."

Speechless, he whirled around. They were standing beneath the apple tree in Soc's front yard!

Smiling, Socrates said, "If you run, you can still make it home for lunch."

Danny shook the mud off his shoes and stepped through his front door. He half expected his parents to run to him, frantic but happy, asking where he had been. But his father only glanced up and smiled. His mother entered the room, took one look at him, and said, "I don't know *how* boys get so dirty! Danny Morgan, you wash up if you want lunch."

"Yes, Mom," said Danny brightly, and he headed for the sink.

While they were eating, Danny said, "Thanks for the lunch, Mom—it's delicious. And, Dad, are there any chores I can help with when we're done?"

His parents looked at each other, then at their son. They both spoke at once. "Are you feeling okay, Danny?"

Danny thought about his quest for the crystal castle. Then he smiled. "I feel just fine" was all he said.

All children are seeds from the stars who look to adults for love, inspiration, guidance, and the promise of a safe and friendly world. We dedicate Starseed Press to this vision and to the sacred child in each of us.

Hal and Linda Kramer,
Publishers

Text Copyright © 1992 by Dan Millman.
Illustrations Copyright © 1992 by T. Taylor Bruce.

H J Kramer Inc
P.O. Box 1082
Tiburon, CA 94920

Library of Congress Cataloging-in-Publication Data

Millman, Dan.
    Quest for the crystal castle : a peaceful warrior children's book
/ Dan Millman : illustrated by T. Taylor Bruce.
    p. cm.
    Summary: Unappreciative of what he has in life, Danny travels with the magical old man Socrates into another world, where his quest for the crystal castle teaches him that it is the journey itself that makes a warrior, not the reward.
    ISBN 0-915811-41-3 : $14.95
    [1. Conduct of life—Fiction. 2. Fantasy.] I. Bruce, T. Taylor, ill. II. Title.
PZ7.M6395Qu 1992
[Fic]—dc20   92-70302
                                                         CIP
                                                          AC

Editor: Robert San Souci
Art Director: Linda Kramer
Editorial Assistant: Nancy Grimley Carleton
Book Production: Schuettge and Carleton
Composition: Classic Typography
Printed in Singapore
10 9 8 7 6